A B, Christopher Bear

STEPHANIE JEFFS
ILLUSTRATED BY JACQUI THOMAS

When Joe woke up, he felt all cross inside.
He did not want to get dressed.
Christopher Bear sat on Joe's bed and
smiled his crooked smile made of button thread.
Joe put a sock over Christopher Bear's head.
"Oh, Joe," said Mom.
"Hurry up and get dressed."

4

6

 At breakfast, Joe felt cross.
He dropped his spoon under his chair.
Then he spilled his juice.
"Oh, Joe," said Mom. "What a mess."

7

After breakfast, Joe cut the fur on Christopher
Bear's tummy with some scissors.
Then he threw Christopher Bear down the stairs.
He didn't care.
"Oh, Joe," sighed Mom.

9

"Hurry up," said Mom,
"we'll be late for preschool."
Joe made a face and dragged his feet.
"Why are you so cross this morning?"
asked Mom.
"I'm not cross," shouted Joe.
But inside he knew he was.
On the way out of the house,
Joe shoved Christopher Bear
headfirst into a boot and left him there.

11

At preschool, Joe pushed past
Jessie and Elizabeth to get to his
table.

Harry was drawing a picture.
Joe snatched Harry's crayons
and drew a horrible scribble
on Ben's paper.

13

Then Joe went to the playhouse.
Jessie and Elizabeth were playing inside.
Joe looked through the window
and stuck out his tongue.
Jessie began to cry.

15

"Joe!" said Miss Rosie. "Come here!
You have been cross all morning,
and now you have been horrible to Jessie.
Sit down here and think about
what you have done."
Joe looked at his shoes.
They were on the wrong feet.
He said nothing.

18

Joe sat and thought.
Suddenly he thought about Christopher Bear,
upside down in a boot, all alone.
Joe started to cry.
He didn't feel cross any more.
Instead, he felt sorry.
He wanted to feel all right again.

"I'm sorry," whispered Joe.

19

Miss Rosie gave Joe a tissue, and held his hand.

"Go and say you're sorry to Jessie," she said.

"I'm sorry," said Joe.

"That's okay," said Jessie. She smiled.

Joe felt a bit happier.

He began to draw a picture.

Miss Rosie smiled at him.

Joe began to feel better.

21

"Everybody to the story mat!" said Miss Rosie.
And so Joe sat down with Jessie on one side
and Ben on the other.

Miss Rosie told a funny story
and everybody laughed, even Joe.
They laughed so much they couldn't stop.
"Time to go home now!" laughed Miss Rosie.

When Mom came to collect Joe from preschool,
she was carrying Christopher Bear.

He looked at Christopher Bear's bald tummy.
"I'm sorry," he whispered.
And he held him very, very tight.
On the way home, Joe told Mom about preschool,
and then he said he was sorry to Mom.
24

At home, Joe snuggled into Mom's lap.

"Joe," said Mom, "shall we say we're sorry to God, too?"

"Why?" asked Joe.

"Well," said Mom, "God's sad when we hurt people."

"Is he cross?" asked Joe.

"God's a bit like Miss Rosie," Mom replied.

"When we say we're sorry, he forgives us.

Then he forgets we have ever been naughty."

Joe closed his eyes, and so did Christopher Bear.
"Father God," said Mom, "we're sorry
for the bad things we have done today.
Thank you that you still love us."
Joe opened his eyes.
Everything was going to be all right.
And Christopher Bear just smiled
his crooked smile made of button thread.

29

Large-quantity purchases or custom editions of this book are available at a discount from the publisher. For more information, contact the sales department at Augsburg Fortress, Publishers, 1-800-328-4648, or write to: Sales Director, Augsburg Fortress, Publishers, P.O. Box 1209, Minneapolis, MN 55440-1209.

First Augsburg Books edition. Originally published as *A Bad Day for Christopher Bear* copyright © 2002 AD Publishing Services Ltd. 1 Churchgates, The Wilderness, Berkhamsted, Herts HP4 2UB

ISBN 0-8066-4367-6
AF 9-4367
First edition 2002

02   03   04   05   06   1   2   3   4   5   6   7   8   9   10